The Declaration of Independence

The Declaration of Independence

Dennis Brindell Fradin

mc Marshall Cavendish
Benchmark
New York

Marshall Cavendish Benchmark
99 White Plains Road
Tarrytown, NY 10591
www.marshallcavendish.us

Text and maps copyright © 2007 by Marshall Cavendish Corporation
Maps by XNR Productions

All Internet sites were available and accurate when sent to press.

Library of Congress Cataloging-in-Publication Data

Fradin, Dennis B.
The Declaration of Independence / Dennis Brindell Fradin.
p. cm. — (Turning points in U.S. history)
Includes bibliographical references and index.
ISBN-13: 978-0-7614-2129-0
ISBN-10: 0-7614-2129-7
1. United States. Declaration of Independence—Juvenile literature. 2. United States—Politics and government—1775–1783—Juvenile literature.
I. Title. II. Series: Fradin, Dennis B. Turning points of United States history.
E221.F815 2006
973.3'13—dc22
2005016023

Photo Research by Connie Gardner

Cover Photo: Bettmann/CORBIS
Title Page: Royalty Free/CORBIS
The photographs in this book are used by permission and through the courtesy of: *The Granger Collection*: 6, 8, 10, 11, 15, 16, 18 (R and L), 34, 36;
Getty Images: Stock Montage, 9; Hulton Archive, 14, 24, 27; Herbert Orth/Time Life Pictures, 28; MPI, 30, 33, 35. *Corbis*: Bettmann, 20, 21, 32.

Editorial Director: Michelle Bisson
Art Director: Anahid Hamparian
Printed in China
3 5 6 4 2

Contents

A stamp tax agent for the British is strung up on a pole in a demonstration against the Stamp Act of 1765. This colored engraving was painted by John Trumbull in 1795.

CHAPTER ONE

The "Hobgoblin" Independence

Between 1607 and 1733, England settled or seized control of thirteen **colonies** in what is now the United States. For many years the colonists had few complaints about British rule.

Trouble broke out in the 1760s and early 1770s when England, needing money, began taxing the colonists on items such as paper goods, glass, paint, and tea. Americans from New Hampshire to Georgia **protested** that "taxation without representation is **tyranny**." This meant that since Americans were excluded from the British government, Britain had no right to taxation. Women calling themselves the Daughters of Liberty refused to buy British goods. Men known as the Sons of Liberty destroyed British property.

The Boston Tea Party of 1773 started the colonists on the road to revolution.

Colonists in Boston, Massachusetts, protested the **tax** on tea by dumping 342 chests of British tea into the harbor. This event became known as the Boston Tea Party.

Taxes weren't the only source of unrest. Having built homes and towns in the wilderness, some colonists were beginning to feel like a separate people rather than **transplanted** English men and women. The first well-known Americans to favor **independence** were Samuel Adams of Massachusetts and Patrick Henry of Virginia. Both men favored separation from England by about 1765. In 1774 John Hancock of Massachusetts suggested that Americans form a new, separate nation called the United States of America. That year, Thomas Jefferson,

This portrait shows Samuel Adams, a delegate to both Continental Congresses, a signer of the Declaration of Independence, and the governor of Massachusetts from 1794–1797.

a tall, redheaded Virginian, made a similar proposal in his pamphlet, *A Summary View of the Rights of British America.*

On the advice of Benjamin Franklin of Pennsylvania, colonial leaders met in Philadelphia in September of 1774 to discuss the troubles with England.

Patrick Henry is famous for the phrase, "Give me liberty or give me death!"

George Washington is shown accepting the office of Commander-in-Chief to the Continental Congress on June 15, 1775, in an 1876 lithograph by Currier & Ives.

Every colony but Georgia sent delegates to the meeting, which was called the First **Continental Congress**. Most of the **delegates**—as was true of most Americans in 1774—hoped to settle the dispute with Britain.

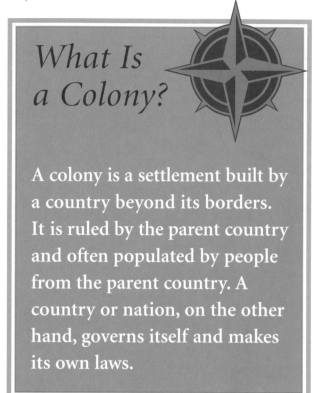

What Is a Colony?

A colony is a settlement built by a country beyond its borders. It is ruled by the parent country and often populated by people from the parent country. A country or nation, on the other hand, governs itself and makes its own laws.

The First Continental Congress sent petitions to Britain demanding fairer treatment. But in case war broke out, Congress told all thirteen colonies to prepare their militias (emergency troops). Before **adjourning** in October, the congressmen agreed to meet in Philadelphia, Pennsylvania, again the next spring if Britain rejected their demands.

Instead of making peace, the British planned a double blow against the colonists. On the night of April 18, 1775, seven hundred British soldiers planned to march out of Boston. Their goal was to capture the rebel leaders, Adams and Hancock, in Lexington, Massachusetts, then seize American military supplies in nearby Concord.

Americans in Boston discovered the British plan and sent Paul Revere on a thirteen-mile (twenty-one km) ride to Lexington. Revere warned Adams and Hancock to flee and alerted Lexington's militia to prepare to fight. Seventy militiamen faced the British force that entered Lexington

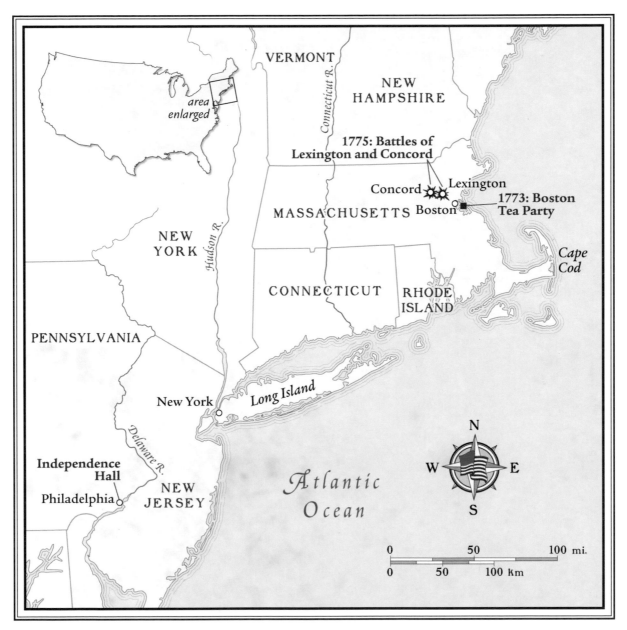

The Fight for Independence

at dawn on April 19, 1775. The British won the Battle of Lexington, which began the Revolutionary War. But as news of the British attack spread, thousands of Americans headed toward Concord. The Americans won the Battle of Concord, which was the first American victory of the war.

Minutemen face British soldiers on Lexington Common, Massachusetts, in the first battle of the War for Independence.

Paul Revere's famous freedom ride is portrayed on this 1905 sheet music cover.

This colored engraving by Francois Xavier Habermann shows people pulling down the statue of King George III in New York on July 9, 1776.

The Second Continental Congress opened in Philadelphia on May 10, 1775. Despite the battles of Lexington and Concord, most Americans were not ready to declare independence. England was the world's mightiest nation. How could America win its independence from such a powerful country? By early 1776, most congressmen considered independence a "frightful hobgoblin" that could bring ruin to America, as Massachusetts delegate John Adams put it.

COMMON SENSE;

ADDRESSED TO THE

INHABITANTS

OF

AMERICA,

On the following interesting

SUBJECTS.

I. Of the Origin and Design of Government in general,
with concise Remarks on the English Constitution.

II. Of Monarchy and Hereditary Succession.

III. Thoughts on the present State of American Affairs.

IV. Of the present Ability of America, with some miscellaneous Reflections.

Man knows no Master save creating HEAVEN,
Or those whom choice and common good ordain.

THOMSON.

PHILADELPHIA;
Printed, and Sold, by R. BELL, in Third-Street.

MDCCLXXVI.

Thomas Paine's book,
Common Sense, was the
first American best-seller.

CHAPTER TWO

"When in the Course of Human Events"

In the first half of 1776, a growing number of Americans became convinced that the time for independence had come. A booklet written by an Englishman who had moved to Philadelphia helped sway public opinion. *Common Sense* by Thomas Paine appeared in January of 1776. Paine's forty-seven-page pamphlet presented simple reasons why America should declare itself independent. For example, since a continent couldn't be ruled by an island forever, putting off independence would just leave the struggle to later Americans. At a time when the total population of all thirteen colonies was only 2.5 million, *Common Sense* sold an amazing half-million copies. It convinced many readers that separation from England was the best course.

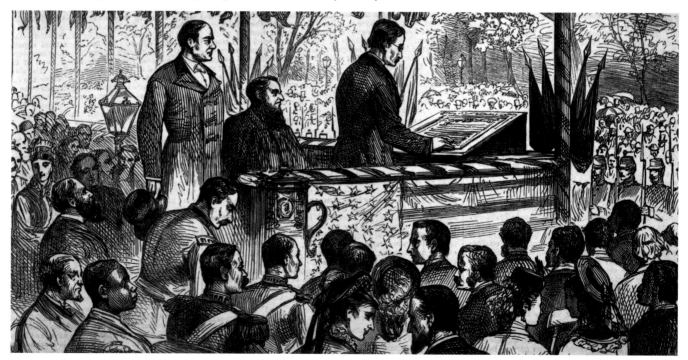

Another factor was that by 1776 America had been fighting England for a year with no end in sight. To win the war, America would probably need the help of other nations. Other countries were reluctant to help a bunch of rebels. However, they might help a people who declared that they were fighting to form a new country.

On June 7, 1776, Richard Henry Lee, a Virginia delegate, rose in Congress and read a proposal: "That these United Colonies are, and of right ought to be, free and independent States." The congressmen decided to vote on Lee's independence proposal in early July.

Richard Henry Lee reads the Declaration of Independence to a group of military officials and civilians on July 4, in Philadelphia, where the Declaration was signed.

If the vote came out for independence, Congress would need a **document** telling the world why America was separating from England. Thomas Jefferson was chosen to write the document. The tall, quiet Virginian sat down at his portable desk in his Philadelphia apartment. Jefferson used no reference books, but blended his own phrases and ideas with those he had encountered in his reading.

"When in the course of human events," he began, "it becomes necessary for one people to dissolve the political bands which have connected them with another . . ." Jefferson became more inspired as his pen moved on. "We hold these truths to be

Thomas Jefferson reads the rough draft of the Declaration of Independence to Benjamin Franklin in this illustration based on a painting by Clyde O. DeLand.

"Tall Tom"

At a time when the average man stood five feet six inches tall, Thomas Jefferson was six feet two. He was called "Tall Tom" as a young man. Among his many achievements besides writing the Declaration of Independence, he served as vice president of the United States from 1797 to 1801 and as the nation's third president from 1801 to 1809. He also designed the Virginia statehouse in Richmond, founded the University of Virginia, and was nicknamed "Mr. Mammoth" because he collected prehistoric bones.

self-evident, that all men are created equal . . ." he wrote, a few lines into his paper. He also explained how Britain had mistreated the colonies. He ended with a stirring sentence: "And for the support of this **Declaration** . . . we mutually pledge to each other our lives, our fortunes, and our sacred honor." Jefferson wrote the entire **Declaration of Independence** in two weeks during late June of 1776. He showed it to Benjamin Franklin and John Adams, who made a few editorial changes.

Only if independence was approved would Congress issue the Declaration. If the measure was voted down, the paper would go out with the trash. Each colony had sent delegates to Congress. If a colony had seven delegates in Congress, four would have to vote for independence for that colony to choose independence.

The Thirteen Colonies

A majority of the colonies—seven out of thirteen—would have to vote for independence for the measure to pass.

Thomas Jefferson counted six colonies that were not yet ready for independence as of June 1776. As July approached, America was at a crossroads. If just one colony that had favored separation from Britain changed its vote, independence would be rejected. America would remain the thirteen English colonies instead of declaring itself to be the United States of America.

Josiah Bartlett was one of the signers of the Declaration of Independence. He went on to become the first governor of New Hampshire.

CHAPTER THREE

"The Future Happiness of America"

On July 1, the day before the official vote, Congress debated independence and voted informally to see how matters stood. For those favoring independence, the news was good. Nine colonies voted for separation from England on July 1. The measure seemed certain to pass when the official vote was made the next day.

But then the delegates in favor of independence realized that they had a serious problem. If nine colonies voted to form a new country, what would become of the four colonies that didn't? Would they remain loyal to England? Might the colonies end up fighting each other? Besides, other nations might not aid a new nation that wasn't united. Somehow a way had to be found to

The First Signer

As president of Congress, John Hancock signed the Declaration first. While signing, he reportedly said: "There! John Bull [a nickname for Britain] can read my name without spectacles and may double his reward on my head!" Because Hancock signed the Declaration first, his signature became famous. Today, people still say "Put your John Hancock there" when requesting a person's signature.

bring the last four colonies over to independence. As New Hampshire delegate Josiah Bartlett wrote to a friend on the eve of the big vote: "It is a Business of the greatest importance as the future happiness of America will Depend on it."

Each of the four colonies not yet in favor of independence faced an obstacle. Leaders in New York had told their delegates not to vote one way or the other on the independence question. One of Delaware's delegates wanted independence and one was against it. The colony's third delegate, Caesar Rodney, favored independence. However, he was 80 miles (129 km) away in Delaware—a long distance to travel in those days. Things looked especially bleak for Pennsylvania and South Carolina. In both those cases, the majority of their delegates opposed independence.

The men who were for independence swung into action. A messenger was sent to inform Rodney that he was needed in Philadelphia to break Delaware's 1–1 tie. Although he was suffering from cancer, Rodney immediately set out in a desperate effort to reach Philadelphia in less than a day. Perhaps traveling partly on horseback and partly by carriage, Rodney journeyed all night through the rain. Meanwhile, Samuel Adams and other pro-independence delegates tried to persuade some wavering colleagues to vote for separation from England.

The day of decision arrived: July 2, 1776. The nine colonies that had voted for independence a day earlier remained steadfast. Two foes of independence from Pennsylvania, Robert Morris and John Dickinson, decided not to vote.

Caesar Augustus Rodney swung Delaware's vote toward independence, helping to make the vote unanimous.

CAESAR RODNEY ARRIVING AT INDEPENDENCE HALL
PHILADELPHIA, IS GREETED BY THOMAS McKEAN
JULY 4TH 1776

This engraving shows Caesar Rodney and Thomas McKeen (left) arriving at Independence Hall to vote in favor of independence.

This enabled Pennsylvania to squeak by for independence by a vote of 3–2. Delaware chose independence when Rodney, wet and exhausted from his all-night journey, arrived in the nick of time to swing his colony's vote. To avoid having their colony stand alone, South Carolina's delegates changed their vote to independence. New York did not vote on July 2, but made the independence vote **unanimous** soon after.

With the July 2 vote, two things happened. The thirteen colonies passed out of existence and the United States was born.

DECLARATION OF INDEPENDENCE
In Congress 4th July, 1776.

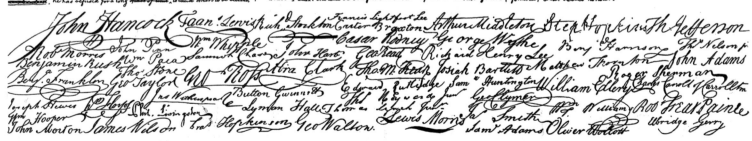

The final version of the Declaration of Independence, signed by all fifty-six members of Congress.

CHAPTER FOUR

The Best-Loved Document in U.S. History

Now that the vote had come out in favor of separation from England, Congress prepared to issue the Declaration of Independence. The congressmen made some changes in Thomas Jefferson's document, and approved it on July 4. Copies of the Declaration were printed and sent out to the thirteen new states. Most members of Congress didn't sign a copy of the Declaration until August 2, 1776, and some signed even later. Delegates to Congress were constantly being replaced. As a result, some of the signers of the Declaration had not been among those who had approved it on July 4.

The Declaration gave Americans something important to fight for: their own country. And as a country, the United States could make **alliances** with other nations. France entered the war on the United States' side in 1778, followed by Spain in 1779 and the Netherlands in 1780.

French Lieutenant General Lafayette leads American troops against the British in the battle of 1777–1778.

Fighting alone, the United States might have lost the war and once again become colonies. But Britain could not defeat the United States *and* its **allies**. France's aid was especially crucial. French troops and ships helped the United States win the war's final battle at Yorktown, Virginia, in the fall of 1781. In the peace **treaty** signed in Paris two years later, Britain recognized that the United States had won its independence.

Comte de Rochambeau (1725–1807) was a crucial ally in America's fight against the British. In this sketch, General Rochambeau reviews his troops before the siege of Yorktown.

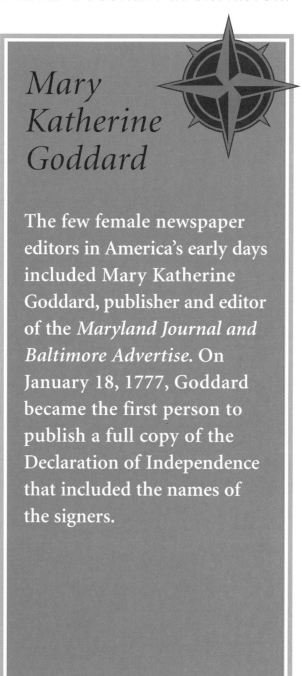

Mary Katherine Goddard

The few female newspaper editors in America's early days included Mary Katherine Goddard, publisher and editor of the *Maryland Journal and Baltimore Advertise.* On January 18, 1777, Goddard became the first person to publish a full copy of the Declaration of Independence that included the names of the signers.

Pomp and Parade

John Adams of Massachusetts wrote to his wife Abigail that July 2, the day of the independence vote, should be celebrated "with pomp and parade, with shows, games, sports, bells, bonfires, from one end of this continent to the other, from this time forward for evermore." Americans do celebrate independence in the ways John Adams predicted, only they do so on the Fourth of July rather than on July 2. Adams later served as the nation's second president.

This French bronze medal, struck in 1783, commemorates the colonists' victories at Saratoga and Yorktown.

An artist's portrayal of the surrender of the British forces by Major General Charles O. Hara at Yorktown, Virginia.

The founders of the country thought that July 2 would be considered the nation's birthday. After all, that was the date they had voted to form a new country. But what happened was that Americans fell in love with the Declaration of Independence. And because at the top of the Declaration it said "JULY 4, 1776"—the date Congress approved the document—Americans began celebrating July 4 instead of July 2 as the nation's birthday.

Definitive treaty of peace with G.B. part.
3. Sept. 1783

Duplicate.

45

In the Name of the most. Holy and undivided Trinity:

It having pleased the Divine Providence to dispose the Hearts of the most Serene and most potent Prince George the Third, by the Grace of God, King of Great Britain, France and Ireland, Defender of the Faith, Duke of Brunswick and Luneburg, Arch Treasurer and Prince Elector of the Holy Roman Empire &c.ª And of the United States of America, to forget all past Misunderstandings and Differences that have unhappily interrupted the good Correspondence and Friendship which they mutually wish to restore, and to establish such a beneficial and satisfactory Intercourse, between the two Countries upon the Ground of reciprocal Advantages and mutual Convenience as may promote and secure to both perpetual Peace & Harmony, and having for this desirable End already laid the Foundation of Peace and Reconciliation by the Provisional Articles signed at Paris on the 30.ᵗʰ of November 1782, by the Commissioners empowered on each Part, which Articles were agreed to be inserted in and to constitute the Treaty of Peace proposed to be concluded between the Crown of Great Britain a

The first page of the Treaty of Paris, signed September 3, 1783. This made the United States official!

The **Fourth of July**, also known as Independence Day, is celebrated as the United States' birthday to this day.

The Declaration of Independence also is still the most famous expression of what the United States stands for. It reminds us that it is wrong to be **prejudiced** against people because of their color or faith, for all people "are created equal." And it inspires us to build a world in which everyone will enjoy the basic freedoms Thomas Jefferson described: the rights to "life, liberty, and the pursuit of happiness."

Glossary

adjourn—To end a meeting or suspend it until a later time.

alliance—Agreement of friendship between countries.

allies—Countries that are friendly.

colony—A settlement built by a country beyond its borders.

Continental Congress—A body of lawmakers that governed the country before the creation of the United States Congress.

declaration—Announcement.

Declaration of Independence—The paper, issued in 1776, announcing that the thirteen colonies had become the United States of America— and why.

delegates—People who act for other people.

document—An official paper.

Fourth of July—The date in 1776 that Congress approved the Declaration of Independence, celebrated as the birthday of the United States.

independence—Freedom, or self-government.

prejudice—A preconceived and unfair opinion not based on facts.

protest—To object to something through words and actions.

self-evident—Plainly seen or known.

tax—Many people are required to pay this to finance the government.

transplanted—Moved to another place.

treaty—An agreement often made to establish or preserve peace.

tyranny—Unjust and oppressive power.

unanimous—Having the support or vote of all.

Timeline

1607—Virginia became England's first permanent American colony

1620—The Pilgrims settle at Plymouth, Massachusetts, beginning England's second permanent American colony

1733—Georgia becomes England's thirteenth American colony

1765—Americans rebel against Britain's Stamp Act tax

1774—First Continental Congress opens on September 5

1775—**April 19:** Revolutionary War begins at Lexington and Concord in Massachusetts
May 10: Second Continental Congress opens

1773—Boston Tea Party is held to protest the British Tea Act

1607   *1765*   *1775*

1776—June 7: Richard Henry Lee of Virginia proposes independence in Congress

July 2: Congress approves independence

July 4: Declaration of Independence, written by Thomas Jefferson, is approved by Congress

1778—France enters the war on the side of the United States, thanks partly to the Declaration of Independence

1779—Spain enters the war on the side of the United States

1780—The Netherlands enters the war on the side of the United States

1781—Major Revolutionary War fighting ends with the victory of the United States at Yorktown, Virginia

1783—By the Treaty of Paris, Britain recognizes that the United States has won its independence

2001—On July 4, the United States celebrates its 225th birthday

1776   *1780*   *2001*

Further Information

BOOKS

Brenner, Barbara. *If You Were There in 1776.* New York: Bradbury, 1994.

Freedman, Russell. *Give Me Liberty!: The Story of the Declaration of Independence.* New York: Holiday House, 2000.

Nardo, Don. *The Declaration of Independence: A Model for Individual Rights.* San Diego, CA: Lucent, 1999.

Oberle, Lora Polack. *The Declaration of Independence.* Mankato, MN: Bridgestone, 2002.

Quiri, Patricia Ryon. *The Declaration of Independence.* New York: Children's Press, 1998.

W E B   S I T E S

Biographies of the signers of the Declaration of Independence
http://www.colonialhall.com/biodoi.asp

Information on the Declaration of Independence and its signers
http://www.ushistory.org/declaration

National Archives electronic exhibit hall on the Declaration of Independence
http://www.archives.gov/exhibit_hall/charters_of_freedom/
    declaration/declaration.html

Bibliography

Bakeless, John, and Katherine Bakeless. *Signers of the Declaration.* Boston: Houghton Mifflin, 1969.

Becker, Carl. *The Declaration of Independence: A Study in the History of Political Ideas.* New York: Knopf, 1960 (reprint).

Brodie, Fawn M. *Thomas Jefferson: An Intimate History.* New York: Norton, 1974.

Donovan, Frank. *Mr. Jefferson's Declaration.* New York: Dodd, Mead, 1968.

Hawke, David. *A Transaction of Free Men: The Birth and Course of the Declaration of Independence.* New York: Scribners, 1964.

Malone, Dumas. *The Story of the Declaration of Independence.* New York: Oxford University Press, 1954.

Index

Page numbers in **boldface** are illustrations.

About the Author

Dennis Fradin is the author of 150 books, some of them written with his wife, Judith Bloom Fradin. Their recent book for Clarion, *The Power of One: Daisy Bates and the Little Rock Nine*, was named a Golden Kite Honor Book. Another of Dennis's recent books is *Let It Begin Here! Lexington & Concord: First Battles of the American Revolution*, published by Walker. The Fradins are currently writing a biography of social worker and anti-war activist Jane Addams for Clarion and a nonfiction book about a slave escape for National Geographic Children's Books. Turning Points in U.S. History is Dennis Fradin's first series for Marshall Cavendish Benchmark. The Fradins have three grown children and three young grandchildren.